The Warli Tribe

कथन

Written by Hye-eun Shin
Illustrated by Su-bi Jeong
Edited by Joy Cowley

जाति
Tribe

In about the 10th century BC,
in the Tanai area of Western India,
there lived a tribe called the Warli.
The women in the Warli tribe
drew pictures on the walls
of their mud-brick houses.
Drawing pictures on mud walls
was a sacred ritual for Warli people.

big & SMALL

Original Korean text by Hye-eun Shin
Illustrations by Su-bi Jeong
Korean edition © Yeowon Media Co., Ltd.

This English edition published by Big & Small in 2014
by arrangement with Yeowon Media Co., Ltd.
English text edited by Joy Cowley
English edition © Big & Small 2014

ISBN: 978-1-921790-92-8

Printed in Korea

उगना

Spring

When spring arrived,
the Warli people
worked in their fields
along the banks of a river.

अंकुर

Planting Seeds

At the beginning of a new year,
the Warli people held a ceremony
to honour the earth,
then they planted seeds.
The seeds were scattered
over all the fields
and covered with earth.

Hunting मृगया

When the men went to the forest,
the animals ran away,
but the men chased them.
Animals provided meat for the tribe
to eat with their grain.

नमक

Getting Salt

The Warli people living by the sea,
also caught and ate fish.
They made salt
from sun-dried sea water,
gathering it in baskets.
Salt was thought of as white treasure.

13

अरण्य

The Forest

The children played in the forest,
gathering flowers and fruits
and chasing monkeys
and other small animals.

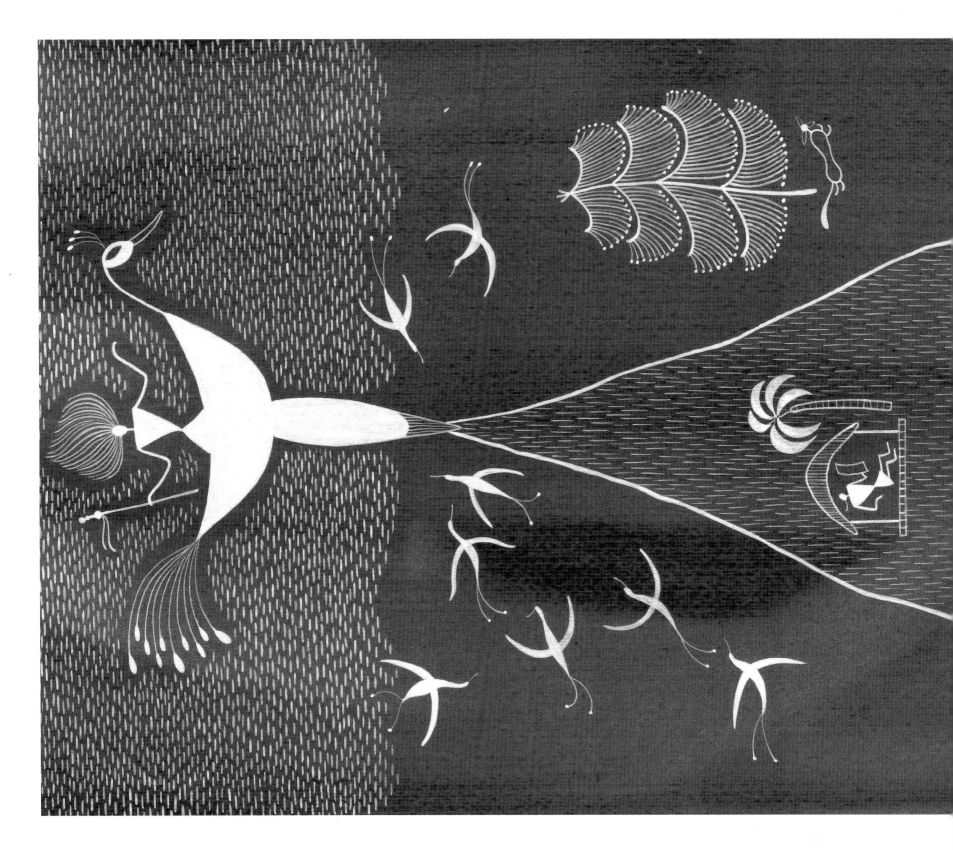

Season of Rain बरसात

In the monsoon season,

heavy rains fell on the earth

and people stayed in their houses.

The rainy season was not a time

to travel or to work in the fields.

बालिका

After the Rain

The streams were full of water
and the river flowed to the sea.
New growth came to the land
after the summer monsoons*.

*The rainy season in India usually starts
in June and lasts until October.

आतप

Animals and Trees

The rain renewed the forest
and there was food for the animals:
fresh green leaves and fruit.
Birds nested in the trees
and animals gave birth.

शशि

The Warli Village at Night

When the sun went down
and the moon rose in the sky,
the Warli people shared food,
made baskets and cloth,
and told stories before going to bed.

उपज

Harvest Time

The crops were ready.
The people cut their corn and rice
and carried it to their village.
This was food for the coming year.

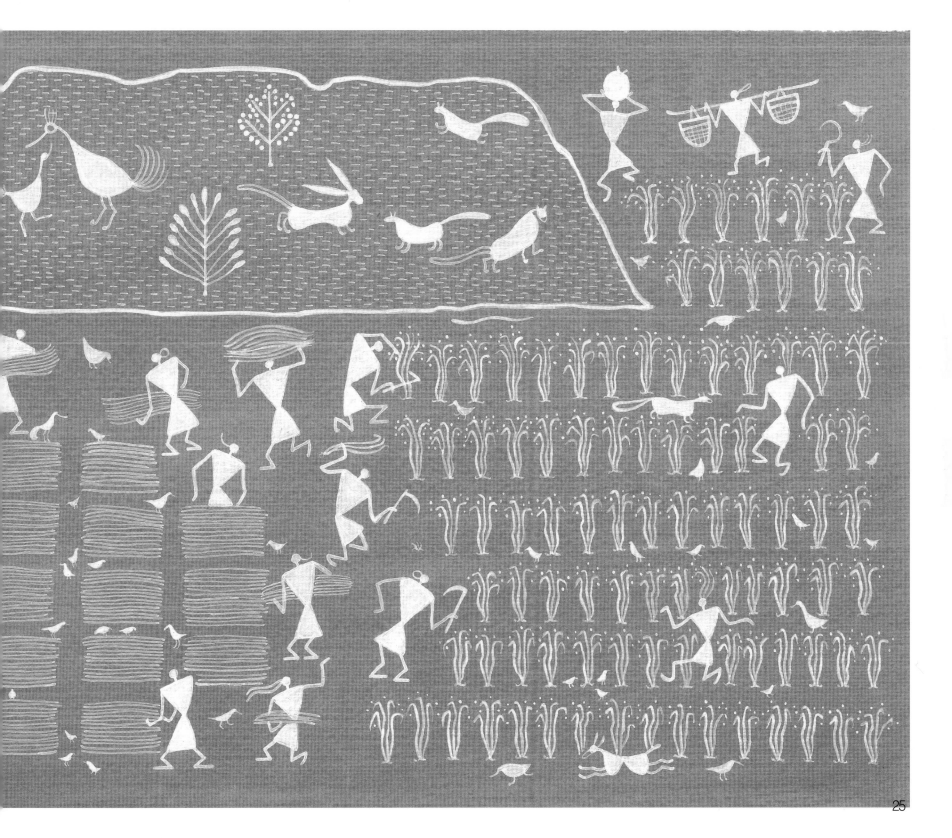

केशकर्तन

Food for the Year

The grain and the stalks
were separated by beating them.
The grain was stored
and the stalks were fed
to the animals.
The seeds were kept for new crops.

शस्यात्सव

Festival Night

When the food was harvested,
the Warli people had a festival.
They danced and sang all night,
celebrating the generosity
of the good earth.

विवाह

Wedding Day

The bride and groom rode a horse
leading a wedding procession.
They were married in the temple
and were ready to start a new family.
The Warli tribe continued with their lives.

The Warli Tribe: Living with Nature

Hello, boys and girls,

Did you enjoy the story about the Warli people?
Our village is in Tanai, in Western India.
The people in the village farm the land for a living.
In spring we plant seeds in the fields.
In summer the rains come.
In autumn, after the rains,
we harvest the ripe grain and store it.
Everyone is happy with the new food
so we have a great festival.
You can see our life story in our art.

Your friend from the Warli tribe

Let's Think

When did farming begin?

How did people's lives change with farming?

How different is farming now, compared to hundreds of years ago?

India: Home of the Warli People

Area: 3,166,414 km²
Capital: New Delhi
Main Languages: Hindi, English

India is located in Asia, with Pakistan to the west, China, Nepal and Bhutan to the north-east, and Bangladesh and Myanmar to the east. India gained independence from the United Kingdom on 15th August 1947. It is the seventh largest country in the world, with the second highest population.

Country of Religions India has many religions – 80 per cent of the population is Hindu, but there are also many Muslims, Jains, Sikhs and Christians. It is where Buddhism first began. For many Indians, religion is a big part of their daily lives.

Economy of India India was one of the first countries in the world to start farming, and nearly 70 per cent of the population are still farmers. The economy grew quickly after independence from the United Kingdom. India is now considered an economic country with strong purchasing power and is the second biggest exporter of software programs.

Warli Painting The Warli people drew pictures on their mud walls with white paint. The drawings look a lot like prehistoric cave paintings. Usually Warli women were the painters, creating pictures about their daily lives.

People around the Indus River

33

Beginning of Farming

Long ago, people wandered the earth looking for food, to hunt or to gather wild grains. Then they found that when the seeds of fruits fell to the ground they grew to produce new fruit, and they discovered farming. This was very important in the change of human civilization because people settled in one place and worked the land. This period was called the New Stone Age.

Rise of Civilization

The first farming started in the Mesopotamian area, between the Tigris and Euphrates rivers. The land between the rivers was very fertile, so farming was easy. Soon farming spread across the world, especially to the four great early settlements: the Mesopotamian civilization, the Egyptian civilization by the Nile River in Egypt, the Indus civilization by the Indus River in India and the Yellow River civilization by the Yellow River in China.

Comb-teeth patterned pottery from the New Stone Age

Ancient Farming

When farming first began, people burned grass and trees to make fields. When the nutrients in the soil disappeared, they would move to another place and start again. This kind of farming was called "slash and burn". People also raised domestic animals and moved on to new pastures. But when populations increased and moving became difficult, people learned to stay in one place for a long time. Farming became a mixture of raising crops and animals.

Effects of Farming

People stopped moving to find food and settled in one place, forming tribes, villages and eventually cities. With improvements in farming techniques, people could produce more food than they needed. People became rich from this excess production. The concept of private property was born, when someone owns a piece of land and all that is on it.

Ancient farming methods

Let's Talk

The things I can do:

1. Learn about farming.

2. Visit a farm.

3. Know where my food comes from.

4. Eat food with thanks to farmers.

5. Join a community garden.

35